For Oscar, with much love.

PUFFIN BOOKS

UK | USA | Canada | Ireland | Australia
India | New Zealand | South Africa

Puffin Books is part of the Penguin Random House group of companies
whose addresses can be found at global.penguinrandomhouse.com.

www.penguin.co.uk   www.puffin.co.uk   www.ladybird.co.uk

Penguin
Random House
UK

First published 2021

001

Text and illustrations copyright © Jion Sheibani, 2021

The moral right of the author/illustrator has been asserted

Text design by Mandy Norman
Printed and bound in China by RR Donnelley Asia Printing Solutions Limited

A CIP catalogue record for this book is available from the British Library

ISBN: 978–0–241–43861–9

All correspondence to:
Puffin Books
Penguin Random House Children's
One Embassy Gardens, 8 Viaduct Gardens
London, SW11 7BW

THE WORRIES

SOHAL FINDS A FRIEND

Written and illustrated by
JION SHEIBANI

PUFFIN

Sohal was full of worries. He had been for as long as he could remember. His parents and teachers often called him 'a worrier', but he wasn't really sure what that meant. It didn't sound good, though, and this made Sohal worry even more.

The worst time for worries was at bedtime, when it felt like the darkness outside Sohal's window was inside his tummy. As soon as Sohal tried to fall asleep the darkness would grow and grow, until it filled every part of his body. It made him toss and turn and **wriggle** and **itch**. It made the worries in his head spin faster and grow **BIGGER**, until he felt like the only thing he could do was cry.

'Don't worry, darling!' said his mum one night. 'Relax! I'll sing you a song! *Twinkle, twinkle, little staaaaar —*'

'No! I don't want that song!' Sohal sulked. 'It's babyish! The only music I like is rap.'

'Right . . . well, why don't we try some calming breathing?' Dad said in his chirpiest voice. 'That's what we do in my yoga class. Just breathe **in** . . .

Breathe **out** . . .

Breathe **in** . . .

Breathe **out**.

Now spread out like a starfish . . . and imagine . . . you're sinking into the soft, golden sand . . .'

'Sinking?!' Sohal yelped, jerking upright.

3

'I don't want to SINK!'

'OK, OK, let's just . . . count some sheep instead,' Mum said quickly. 'One, two, three . . .'

Sohal closed his eyes and imagined some nice fluffy sheep jumping over a fence in a sunny green field. However, the nice fluffy sheep quickly turned into . . .

MUTANT ALIEN SHEEP!

And they were running from a

GIANT
ROBOT WOLF!
In a storm!

Sohal cried out and buried his head in Mum's lap. She sighed, and Dad stroked his hair.

The worst thing was that, whenever Sohal did finally fall asleep, his worries would appear even more clearly (and weirdly) in his dreams.

And when Sohal woke up from his bad dreams he felt scared, tired and a little bit miserable. It felt like there was no one he could talk to about his worries. When people asked if he was OK, he couldn't find the words to explain his feelings. So sometimes he'd panic and say something rude, like:

'GET LOST, YOU BIG FAT FARTYPANTS!'

But mostly he said . . .
nothing at all.

This made Sohal feel very alone. Everyone in the world seemed to have friends except him. At least Sohal had his hamster, Ham Solo. Ham had been Sohal's trusty, smelly, squeaky little friend for the past year and seventy-one days. But, sadly, Sohal couldn't take Ham Solo to school.

At break time Sohal would stand on his own in the playground, feeling like an alien on a foreign planet. Everyone belonged to a group. There were:

the KIDS WHO PLAYED FOOTBALL

the Kids Who Played With Insects

the *Kids Who Played With Each Other's Hair*

the *KIDS WHO STALKED THE TEACHER*

Even the **Kids with No Friends** all sat next to each other!

Sohal didn't want to tell his mum and dad about how lonely he was, because he was worried they'd be worried – and there was already a lot of worrying going on!

Then one day Sohal's teacher,
Mrs Cherry, asked him to draw a picture
of something he was worried about. Sohal
began to draw a **monster** . . . and then
another . . . and then **another** . . .

And soon he realized that these were
the worries that chased him around in his
dreams. They looked much less scary on
paper than they did in his head.

So when he got home, Sohal decided
to hang the drawing above his bed to
remind him that his worries weren't
so scary after all.

Then, something very, very
STRANGE happened.

Chapter 2

That night Sohal didn't have any bad dreams. He slept soundly, with a smile as big as a scooped-out moon on his face . . . until he was woken by a loud **SQUEAK**.

At first he thought it was Ham Solo, but the squeak didn't sound . . . hamstery enough. Sohal slowly opened his eyes, and in the glow of his (many) night lights he saw some shadowy shapes at the end of his bed.

Maybe it's Ham Solo with an army of hamster Jedi? Sohal thought. He leaned in closer (but not too close). Then he realized. These weren't hamsters. They were the monsters from his drawing!

But, now that he saw them for real, he saw that they were actually kind of cute.

'Who are you?' Sohal cried.

One of the monsters shuffled forward. Sohal was alarmed to see that it had **SIX** eyes. What on earth did it need **SIX** eyes for?!

'We are your Worries,' the monster said. 'And my name's **HURT**. I worry about, well . . . getting hurt, mainly.'

'Are you real?' Sohal said, pinching himself hard, in case he was still sleeping.

'Well, we're all the things you worry about, so we definitely ARE real, thank you very much,' Hurt said, scratching at a bandage on his head.

big bandage (in case of bumps)

supersonic hearing!

six eyes (to keep watch for danger!)

elbow pads

thick gloves

scar tattoos (don't ask)

plasters (for every tiny scratch)

knee pads

A creature that looked like a furry
octopus came forward next, nudging the
other Worries out of the way with
its tentacles.

funky
bouffant

no-nonsense
eyebrows

loud
mouth

bag of treats
and essentials for
calming all the
Worries

'Excuse me, excuse me – I think you'll find I'm in charge around 'ere,' she said gruffly. 'Allow ME to say hello. I'm **BABS**. Nice to meet ya, darlin'. I look after all them Worries.' Babs pointed to the creatures sitting behind her.

lots of extendable tentacles for keeping the Worries in line

Sohal frowned. 'So, you're not a Worry yourself, then?'

'Oh yeah, I am!' said Babs proudly. 'I'm just **LOTS** of Worries all at once. You know that weird feelin' in yer tummy when you can't quite put yer finger on what's worryin' ya?'

'Yes!' Sohal said. 'I get that ALL the time!'

'Well, that's me! I'm the one who figures out which of these squirts needs attention.'

'Hey, who you calling squirt?' a third Worry piped up. She was much smaller than Babs. She also had pointy ears on the top of her head and sharp little teeth.

'Don't start, Ang,' Babs warned, raising a furry tentacle. 'Listen, why don't you lot do somefink useful and introduce yerselves to the lad?'

Babs started lining up the Worries on the bed in front of Sohal. They **wriggled** and **squirmed** and **squeaked** in protest before eventually giving in to her many-tentacled grip.

It's a bit like watching hopeless auditions for a TV talent show, thought Sohal. Ham Solo, meanwhile, was fascinated.

'I suppose I'll go first then, as none of the rest of you have got the guts,' the small

monster said, rolling her eyes. 'Yo, I'm **ANGER**. But I'm known as The Ang. When people see me coming, they say,

"DANG! It's The ANG!"

I don't like folks yelling or frowning, or animals with teeth. **Uh-uh**. I got a turquoise belt in karate, judo, aikido, taekwondo, anacondo – you name it. So, if any punk gets mad with me, I get **REAL** mad with them. Know what I'm saying?'

Ang did some air chops and kicked her little legs about.

'Turquoise?' Sohal said. 'That's not a
karate belt colour!'

'**Is too!**' Ang snapped. 'You just ain't
heard of it cos it's so impossible to get.

Hi-yaaaa!
Hi-yyaaa!
HI-YYAAAAAA!'

Sohal watched Ang attempt some painful-looking backflips and decided not to argue. Instead he turned his attention to the next Worry in line, who had a nose that looked like it might **honk** if you squeezed it.

'Hey, I'm **BIG**,' he said. 'I worry about growing up and stuff. I don't like getting dressed or brushing my teeth or any kind of responsibility. No, sir. It gets me all in a **bumfuzzle**! And if I'm gonna be honest . . . I'd like to go back to being a baby and wearing nappies again.'

baseball cap
(to hide greasy hair)

three eyes
(never looking
in the same
direction)

BIG nose
(HONK HONK!)

'cool'
T-shirt

unwashed
fur

overgrown
claws

BIG belly
(will eat
ANYTHING)

thick, snuggly scarf (great for hiding in)

one big eye (for seeing only what is wrong)

skinny, shaky legs (prone to collapsing)

A Worry with one eye was up next. It stood with its head down and its spindly arms hanging awkwardly by its side.

'Hiyaaa. Me name's **FAIL**,' he said in a **trembling** high-pitched voice. 'I worry about getting things wrong. I'm rather good at cheating and keeping me mouth shut for a **REAAAAALLY** long time. Errr . . . that's about it, really!'

The last Worry, the most worried-looking
of all, resembled a ball of dark knotted hair.
All Sohal could see of its face was two wide,
TERRIFIED eyes.

Sohal waited for it to speak. But
the Worry just sat there, frozen to
the spot.

'Ooh, this one's terribly shy,' Babs said,
putting her tentacles on her hips. 'Ya
find it hard to talk to people,
don't ya? Come on, darlin',
tell the lad yer name.'

'I'm **ALONE**,'
the Worry squeaked at long
last. 'I worry about . . . er,

thick, tangled
hair (impossible
to brush)

HUGE
observant
eyes

special rabbit
teddy

well, being alone. I don't like empty places or really crowded places or the dark, but I do like playing on phones and the internet. And –' she paused – 'pickled-onion-flavour Monster Munch.'

'Er, okayyyy,' Sohal said, trying to take in everything he'd heard. 'Well, it was nice to meet you all. But could you . . . go away now, please? I've got to get ready for school in a bit.'

It was still dark outside, but Sohal could hear a dustbin lorry whirring down the street. His mum and dad would be up soon. And what would they do if they saw the Worries?

'Oh no, no, no,' the Worries said. 'We're staying with you!'

'You can't do that!' Sohal said, panicked. 'If anyone at school sees you, they'll make SO much fun of me!'

'Anyone? Who's Anyone? Yo, you let me worry about him!' said Ang, doing some more karate chops.

'Hey! Slow down, all o' ya!' Babs said. 'Yer gonna give the lad a fright. Let's give 'im a chance to get used to us, hey?' She turned to Sohal. 'I'll make sure they don't all come to school wiv' ya, dontcha worry. I'll do ALL the worryin' for ya!'

Sohal looked at Babs smiling up at him.

He started to feel slightly better, but then he remembered that Babs was LOTS of worries all rolled into one. So, even if she did take care of the other Worries, he would still have HER to worry about!

'**Oh no!**' he groaned.

Today was definitely going to be One Of Those Days.

Chapter 3

While Sohal went to the bathroom, the
Worries were under STRICT instructions to
stay where he had shoved them — under his
bed. But, when he got back to his room,
he saw they had disappeared! And so
had his hamster.

Sohal scurried
downstairs.

Sure enough, he found all the Worries in the kitchen, raiding the cupboards.

'What are you DOING?' he hissed. 'I told you to stay under my bed! My mum and dad will be down any MINUTE!'

'But we're

HUNGRYYYYY!'

Hurt whined, clinging to a swinging cupboard door for dear life. 'And now I'm stuck. **HELP!'**

'I did tell you to wait for a grown-up to help us,' Big grumbled.

'And **YOU**, Ham Solo!' Sohal said, pulling his hamster out of a bag of Cheesy Puffs. 'How did you get out of your cage?'

'It was me!' Alone squeaked. 'I couldn't BEAR the thought of him being in there all by himself!'

Sohal spotted Ang attacking the cat
with a dustpan and brush, shouting:

'YO, STAY AWAY
FROM **MY MILK**, YOU
MONSTER!'

'I can't reach the CEREAL!' shrieked Fail, who was balanced on top of a glass, on top of a bowl, on top of a cheese grater. Was it just Sohal's imagination or did Fail somehow seem much **bigger**?

Alone came bouncing towards Sohal. 'I'm so happy to see you!' she squealed. 'I thought you'd left us for EVER!'

'I was only gone for five minutes,' Sohal said moodily.

Alone burst into tears.

'WAAAAAAAAAAH!!!!'

she wailed. 'You hate me, don't you?

WAAAAAH!
BOOOOOO!
WAAAAAAH!'

'Shhhhh! No I don't.' Sohal tried to calm her down. 'I'm sorry, OK? You're . . . great.'

Alone immediately stopped crying, and bounced on to Sohal's head.

'Oh goodyyyy!' she squeaked happily. 'Thank goodness for that!'

Just then, they all heard Sohal's mum and dad coming down the stairs. The Worries quickly shovelled as much food as they could into their mouths, then scrambled for somewhere to hide. Sohal was just thinking how well they were doing when he turned to see Fail on the kitchen counter, staring hopelessly at the piles of cereal around her.

'Oh dear. Oh no!' Fail whined. 'We're going to be in SO much trouble!'

Then, to Sohal's astonishment, Fail began to **grow** . . .
and **grow**!

'NO! You're supposed to be HIDING! Not GROWING!' Sohal yelped.

But, the more Sohal panicked, the bigger Fail seemed to get. And Sohal's parents' footsteps were getting closer and closer . . .

'Hurry uuuup!' Alone squawked, jumping up and down on top of Sohal's head.

Then, just as the kitchen door opened, one of Babs's tentacles shot out from behind the fruit bowl. In a split second it had lassoed

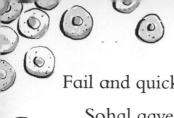

Fail and quickly yanked her to safety.

Sohal gave a huge sigh of relief and collapsed into a chair.

'Morning, love!' Sohal's mum sang out as she came in.

'Oh hi!' said Sohal.

Alone quickly bounced off Sohal's head and into the box of Coco Pops, just before his dad's hand landed in his hair and ruffled his curly locks.

'All right, kiddo?' Dad said sleepily.

Then Sohal's parents saw the mess.

'Sohal! What's all this?' Mum cried.

'It looks like burglars have been for breakfast!' Dad exclaimed.

Sohal gulped, and his eyes
filled with tears. He couldn't think
of an excuse, or a way to explain why
the cat was cowering in the corner, looking
like she'd been frazzled in the toaster.

'Hey, kiddo, don't worry about it,'
Dad said, his voice quickly softening.
'We can clear it up together.'

'Yes, and at least you actually ate some
breakfast for once!' Mum continued. 'I
guess your tummy must be feeling OK this
morning, hey, love?'

In fact, Sohal's tummy was

NOT FEELING OK.

He usually had butterflies in his stomach before he went to school, but today it felt like he had BATS flapping around in there! He wasn't going to tell his mum and dad that, though.

When he'd finished cleaning up, Sohal went upstairs and put Ham back in his cage, then brushed his teeth in two seconds flat. He thought maybe, if he got ready fast enough, he could leave the house without the Worries noticing.

'Gosh, I've never seen you in such a hurry to get to school!' said Mum, as Sohal grabbed his rucksack and flew out of the door.

He looked back to check the
Worries weren't following him.

'Phew,' he muttered, as he
followed his mum
up the hill to
school. 'That
was close.'

WASH YOUR HANDS!
1. Wet your hands
2. Rinse with soap
3. Scrub-a-dub-dub
4. Rinse
5. Dry

happy   excited   sad   angry   frustrated

confused   tired   nervous   curious   ????????

how are you?

YOU ARE A ★

❊ Chapter 4 ✪

DREAM BIG!

At registration that morning Sohal stared
out of the window, wondering what on earth
his Worries could be up to at home.

Then he heard Mrs Cherry's voice saying
his least favourite word in the world: 'PE.'
Oh no! He had forgotten today was PE
day! Maybe that was why all his Worries
had suddenly appeared at once. Sohal *hated*
PE. He wasn't very good at it, and he was

always picked last for teams . . .

There were loud cheers from the rest
of Sohal's class, mainly from a boy called
Chip Monk. Chip was the sportiest boy in
Sohal's class. He was also the loudest.
And the meanest.

'**PE!** PE! **PE!**'

he chanted, banging his fists on the table.

'That's quite enough, Chip,' Mrs Cherry warned.

Sohal started to get a pain in his stomach. He put up his hand to ask to go to the toilet when suddenly he heard a muffled SQUEAK. It was coming from his rucksack! Sohal bent down and opened it – and staring back at him with one big, worried eye was Fail.

'DON'T!' Fail peeped. 'Don't put up your hand! Whatever you say, you'll sound **STUPID**!'

'What are you doing here?' Sohal whispered angrily. 'You're supposed to be at home! Where are the others?'

Just as he asked this, Sohal saw Big

rear up his head,
gasping for air.
Then came Hurt,
elbowing Babs
and Ang out of
his way. And,
squashed right at
the bottom, squealing in
the dark, was Alone.

Without thinking, Sohal
reached in and pulled Alone out, then
slipped her into his shirt pocket before
Mrs Cherry could see.

'Hey, what about US?' Hurt yelped.
'I'm covered in bruises here!'

'I'll deal with you lot later,' Sohal said, zipping his rucksack shut.

Suddenly the class new girl Jazmin, aka Jaz, leaned over towards him. Jaz had been Sohal's desk buddy for weeks now, but he had been too shy to talk to her.

'Dude,' she whispered, 'are you . . . talking to yourself?'

Sohal tried his best to look Absolutely Normal, but Alone was wriggling like crazy in his pocket, which made him feel tickly.

'Err . . . yeah!' he spluttered. He put his

hands over his mouth to stop his laughter, but it was no use. He sounded a lot like a giggling pig.

'**TEEE-HEEE** SNORT! **TEEE-HEEE** SNORT!'

'You are such a weirdo,' Jaz said, smiling. 'But that's cool.'

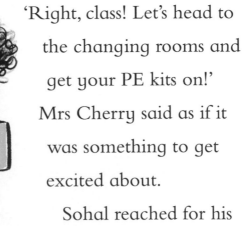

'Right, class! Let's head to the changing rooms and get your PE kits on!' Mrs Cherry said as if it was something to get excited about.

Sohal reached for his

rucksack, his stomach twisting again. Just thinking about PE made his heart pound so fast that Alone couldn't wriggle any more. She was too busy being bumped back and forth by the

thump
thump
thump

of Sohal's chest.

Sohal opened his rucksack ever so carefully in case any of the Worries popped their heads up again. He stuck his hand in to pull out his PE kit, but after some rummaging Sohal realized it WASN'T THERE!

And worse . . . neither were the Worries!

chapter 5

While everyone else went charging towards the changing rooms, Sohal scrambled around on all fours looking for his five furry Worries.

What he *should* have been looking for was five furry Worries dressed in a PE vest . . . a pair of shorts . . . a sock . . . another

sock . . . PE bag . . . and a pair of black plimsolls.

'**THERE THEY ARE!**' squeaked Alone, pointing at her friends from Sohal's shirt pocket.

Sohal turned round and saw his PE kit shuffling towards the door.

He gasped. '**THE WORRIES! NOOooOO!**'

Sohal ran and scooped them up, just before Mrs Cherry stepped on them.

She frowned as Sohal sprang up from the floor. 'Are you all right, Sohal?'

'Yes, fine, miss! I just dropped my kit!'

Mrs Cherry watched Sohal carefully. She could have sworn his plimsolls were wriggling . . . but surely not. She turned and headed out of the classroom.

Sohal stuck his head into his PE bag. 'WHAT were you lot THINKING?' he hissed. 'Someone might have seen you!'

'There was a VERY sharp compass in that rucksack of yours,' Hurt said breathlessly. 'If I'd stayed in there for one more minute

I COULD HAVE DIED!'

'I don't like being at school,' moaned Big. 'It's making me very anxious. I just wanna go home and play with my toys!'

'Well, you can't!' Sohal said sternly. 'You have to stay in my bag for now. And take my PE kit off!'

'**LEAVE 'IM BE!**' Babs yelled, yanking the Worries so they all fell to the bottom of the bag. 'You just get on wiv yer PE class, darlin'. I'll keep 'em quiet.'

Sohal nodded, pulled the drawstring of his PE bag tight shut, then ran to catch up with everyone else.

When he got to the changing rooms, Chip Monk was shouting about how he was

going to thrash everyone because today it was volleyball and he was OBVIOUSLY the **strongest** AND TALLEST AND **fastest** kid in the entire class, blah-blah-blah-blah-blah. Sohal quietly got undressed in a corner and wondered what would be worse: playing ON Chip's team, or playing AGAINST Chip's team.

Suddenly Alone popped up. 'Don't leave me!' she squeaked. 'It stinks in here!

POOOOOOEEEEEE!'

'Oh for goodness' sake!' Sohal whispered, shoving her in his shorts pocket instead. He realized that she barely fit. 'Have you *grown*?'

'No,' she said sheepishly. 'Er . . . maybe?'

'What! So, you Worries . . . you *can* grow?'

Alone gave a nervous chuckle. 'Yes, I think so! The more you worry about me, the bigger I get!'

'Oh brilliant,' Sohal groaned. 'That's all I need!'

Chapter 6

'Who wants to be a team captain?' Mrs Cherry smiled, her eyes sweeping over the class like a torch. Lots of hands flew up. Sohal ducked down. But he knew one of Mrs Cherry's favourite things was choosing people who didn't put their hand up.

'Pleasenotme, pleasenotme, pleasenotme,' he murmured.

Chip waved his arm around in front of Mrs Cherry's face until she had no choice but to give in.

'All right, Chip.' She sighed. 'You can be a team captain. And . . . Jazmin, I don't think you've been captain before?'

Sohal noticed Jaz didn't have her hand up either, but she wasn't hiding like he was.

'Don't think so, miss.' Jaz shrugged. 'I don't mind being one, though.'

She went and stood next to Mrs Cherry, then turned to face Chip, who was pulling silly faces at her. But Jaz just stared at him, hands firmly on her hips. Sohal had never seen anything so **COOL**.

'Captains, choose your teams!'
Mrs Cherry cried. 'Jazmin, you start.'

'OK . . . I pick Sohal,' said Jaz.

Sohal thought he must have heard wrong.
He couldn't have been chosen first! No way.
Uh-uh. That **NEVER** happened.
But then he saw Jaz staring right at him and
making funny 'come-over-here' signs with
her head.

Sohal felt Alone wriggle around in his
pocket. The next thing he knew, she was
sticking her head out and squeaking, 'Sohal,
did she say "Sohal"? Yippeeee! She chose US!'

Sohal quickly pushed Alone back into
his pocket.

As he shuffled up front towards Jaz,
Sohal thought he could see her looking at
him suspiciously. Had she seen Alone?
Sohal slunk behind Jaz and tried to think
about something else.

Jaz continued choosing the other members
of her team. But she didn't choose all her
friends or all the sporty ones, as team captains
normally did. She seemed to be choosing all
the kids who were . . . not good at PE.

This made Chip and his friends laugh.

'So what you gonna call your team,
Jazmin?' he sneered. **'The LOSERS?'**

'Actually, we're the Scaredy Cats,' she
said with a confident smile.

Chip howled with laughter. 'The *Scaredy* Cats! What kind of name is THAT?'

'The kind that admits we might be scared,' Jaz said, taking one step closer to Chip and looking him right in the eye, 'but we are still cats. And cats are **not** to be messed with.'

'Well, in that case, WE are the Lions!' sneered Chip. 'And we will eat you alive!

ROAR!'

'That's enough, Chip,' said Mrs Cherry. 'I want to see friendly competition only, please. Now, team captains, shake hands — and let the game commence!'

chapter 7

Unfortunately, the Scaredy Cats were probably THE worst volleyball team in the history of volleyball. They ran around the gym like headless chickens, some of them dodging the ball like it was a bomb, only to end up flat on their faces.

They were puffing and panting and
sweating all over, but they were always
cheered on by their captain, Jaz. It was
the first time Sohal had truly felt part of a
team – and it was wonderful.

That was, until Alone popped up again.

'OOOOH!

I'm worried!' she
squeaked. 'We don't
seem to be doing very
well. Aren't the rest of
the team going to be
cross with us?'

'Not NOW!' Sohal hissed, waving his arms and trying to whack the speeding ball. It fell to the ground – again. Another point to Chip's team.

'Yeaaaah! Go, LIONS!'

they jeered. 'Too bad, Shorty Sohal!'

'Chip Monk! One more mean word and I'm sending you off the court,' Mrs Cherry snapped.

Suddenly Alone wriggled like crazy.

'I really need a wee-wee!' she whined. 'I **WEE LOADS** when I'm worried! Hurry up, or I'll have to wee here!'

'You can't do that!' Sohal hissed. 'Hold it in for a minute!'

'NO, IT HAS TO BE NOW!'

Just then, Sohal saw something dart across the gym. Was it a mouse? A rat? A ratty mouse? Or, possibly . . . a hamster?

'Ham *Solo!*' Sohal gasped as the creature's fat little body came wiggling fast towards him. 'How did you get here?'

'Ah yes, sorry!' Alone squeaked. 'I forgot to mention we brought Ham too. I just couldn't stand to think of him being by himself ALL DAY!'

'I don't believe this!' Sohal groaned, scooping his hamster up and into his other pocket.

'Everything all right, Sohal?' Mrs Cherry shouted across the gym.

'Er, yes, miss! I just need the toilet.'

Mrs Cherry narrowed her eyes. 'OK . . . Well, off you go!'

Sohal ran towards the door. He heard a yelp, and when he looked down he saw that Alone had grown again, and was now bursting out of his pocket. Sohal cupped his hands over her and flew out of the gym like a missile.

chapter 8

When they got to the toilets, Alone and Ham Solo tumbled out of Sohal's pockets. Alone sat on the floor, taking big, dramatic breaths.

'I told you I do not like small spaces!' she whined. 'Please don't put me back into any kind of pocket again. And no more silly running!'

'Well, it's your fault for coming to school with me. And now I'm missing the rest of the game and letting my team down!' Sohal thought he might cry.

Ham Solo scrambled up Sohal's leg and jumped into his arms. Sohal smiled. Ham always knew exactly when Sohal needed a cuddle. Then Alone jumped on them both.

'Group HUG!' she cried. 'I love group HUuuuUGs!'

'Didn't you need to go to the toilet?' Sohal reminded her.

'Oh YEAH, silly me!' She giggled, and bounced into one of the cubicles.

She was in there for what felt like *hours*. And, when Alone finally did come out, she was covered in toilet paper. It looked like a terrible attempt at an Egyptian mummy costume, but Alone seemed very proud of herself.

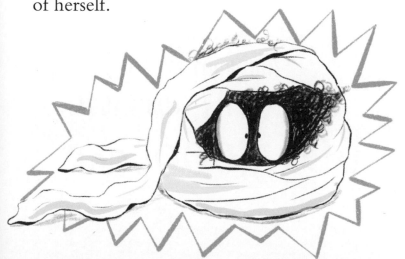

'Is THAT what you were doing all this time?' Sohal said fretfully. He peered behind her into the cubicle. 'There's toilet paper all over the floor and the roll is . . . IN THE TOILET?! Now I'm really in trouble!'

'OOOOH, YOU'RE UPSET!'

Alone wailed.

'YOU WANT ME TO GO AWAY, DON'T YOU? BOOHOOOOOOO!'

Streams of tears began pouring out of her eyes like fountains. What's more, she was getting **bigger** by the second . . .

'Oh no, Alone! Please stop! Please don't grow!' Sohal pleaded. He tried patting her comfortingly on the head, but it didn't do any good. She was still growing!

Suddenly the door of the toilets swung open. Sohal held his breath, expecting to see one of the other boys, or a teacher, or the caretaker, or

GULP

the headmistress . . .

Chapter 9

Sohal gasped. 'You're not meant to be in here! It's the BOYS' toilets!'

At first Jaz didn't say anything. She just looked at the puddles of water and reams of loo paper on the floor, then at Ham Solo peeking out from behind Sohal's leg.

Her eyes widened.

'Looks like me being in the boys' toilets is the least of your worries, dude. What have you been **DOING** in here?!'

Sohal didn't know what to say. He just kept opening and closing his mouth like a strange, curly-haired fish. Why hadn't Jaz said anything about the great big *hairy* monster behind him?

Sohal turned round – and realized Alone had vanished. 'How could she just disappear?' He frowned. 'She was right here!'

'Look, dude, you're making no sense, and I'm not even gonna even ask why you've brought your hamster to school,' said Jaz, 'but we'd better clear this up before Mrs C. comes

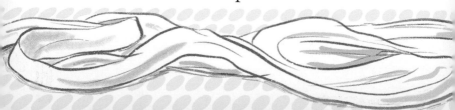

looking for you. As long as that's water, not wee, right? Cos I'm not touching anyone's wee. No way, José!'

'No, ha, no, it's, er, water,' Sohal said, giggling. He wanted to say a lot of other things too, like 'thank you for choosing me to be in your team', 'sorry for running off like a loser', 'you seem cool', and 'could we possibly, maybe be friends?' But every time he tried to speak it felt like he had something stuck in his throat.

Jaz and Sohal used an **INSANE** amount of paper towels to mop up the mess, and even fished the soggy loo roll out of the toilet bowl, squealing the whole time.

(They saw what might have been a tiny speck of poo . . .) Then they raced back to PE together, chattering and laughing the whole way.

Thankfully, Mrs Cherry was so busy telling Chip Monk off that she didn't even notice Jaz and Sohal sneaking back into the gym.

Sohal scanned the room for any sign of Alone, but he couldn't see her.

That's weird, he thought. *Maybe the Worries have finally decided to behave?*

Chapter 10

When the bell for break time rang Sohal changed out of his PE kit as quickly as he could, then opened his bag carefully.

He was almost relieved to see his Worries in there, **squabbling** and **squealing**.

'Oh, thank goodness you're **BACK**!' shouted Hurt.

'Let us out!' Big squeaked. 'It's stuffy in here!'

Sohal did a head count. 'Where's Alone?'

'She was with you!' Babs said. 'Don't tell me you've gone an' lost 'er?!'

Sohal looked worried. 'No, she disappeared in PE . . .'

'**Oh NO!**' cried Fail. 'I can't believe you lost her! That's **TERRIBLE**!'

Sohal was fed up. Nothing was going right today! He thought about going to look for Alone. But then he thought that maybe if he just *ignored* his worries, they might eventually get bored and go away. It was worth a try. So he pulled the drawstring and closed his PE bag, then hung it up on his peg in the corridor.

Sohal decided to spend break time like he always did: sitting on a bench, hiding behind some coats, and looking at his **ALIEN PET SHOP**™ cards. At least he didn't have to look at them on his own today – Ham Solo was with him, so Sohal didn't feel quite as lonely as he usually did.

Sohal had eighty-nine cards in total, and he was very proud of his collection. The problem was, he didn't have anyone to swap his cards with. No one else at his school collected **ALIEN PET SHOP**™ cards any more. Now **BLING-BLING FOOTBALL**™ cards were all the rage.

Sohal liked football, but he pretended he didn't, because he worried he was terrible at it. Besides, he wasn't brave enough to ask anyone to play with him.

While he was looking at card number 134 (Slobba Snail), Sohal heard some kids coming down the corridor. He quickly hid Ham Solo in his pocket again.

Suddenly Jazmin's head appeared through the coats. She grinned at him. 'Hey, dude, what are you hiding here for? Come outside!'

'Er, no thank you. I'm fine.'

Then Jaz spotted what he was holding. 'Ooh, you've got **ALIEN PET SHOP**™ cards! Me TOO!

I've got no one to swap them with – at least, I thought I didn't. I've got a hundred and seventy-six in total,' she said proudly.

Sohal's face lit up like a Christmas tree. 'Wow, that's amazing! I've got eighty-nine. But I'm getting loads more at the weekend when I get my pocket money!'

'Cool! Come outside and show me them!'

Sohal hesitated for a minute. And then, for the first time in weeks, he found himself walking *voluntarily* (that is, without Mrs Cherry dragging him) down the corridor and outside into the playground. Then Sohal and Jaz sat under a tree while he showed her all his best **ALIEN PET SHOP**™ cards.

TIDDLYWINKS
THE MONSTER HEDGEHOG

SUPERPOWER: poison needles
STRENGTH: 84
MAINTENANCE: low

NUTTER
THE THREE-EYED
FLYING SQUIRREL

SUPERPOWER: acorn bomb
STRENGTH: 92
MAINTENANCE: low

POLLY CEPHALUM
THE FOUR-HEADED PARROT

SUPERPOWER: death by talking
STRENGTH: 86
MAINTENANCE: medium

NIGHTMARE BUNNY
THE DROOLING RABID RABBIT

SUPERPOWER: nuclear carrots
STRENGTH: 99
MAINTENANCE: medium

PEEWEE
THE ZOMBIE CHIHUAHUA

SUPERPOWER: toxic poo
STRENGTH: 80
MAINTENANCE: high

SLOBBA SNAIL
THE MUTANT MOLLUSC

SUPERPOWER: deadly mucus
STRENGTH: 78
MAINTENANCE: low

Sohal was having a lot of fun until Jazmin had a terrible idea.

'Let's play football!' she said.

Sohal shook his head. **'NO WAY!'**

'Look, some of my friends are playing now too,' Jaz said, pointing. 'Come on, Sohal! Team Scaredy Cats, remember?'

She put out her hand for a high-five, but Sohal was too busy staring in **terror** at the football pitch. It was full of the usual crowd, but he was mostly worried about Chip Monk and his mates, who were charging around like Vikings.

'Erm, I'll just stay here and watch. You play,' Sohal mumbled. He half expected (and definitely wanted) Jaz to change her mind and stay with him, but she leaped to her feet.

'OK!' she said, grinning. 'Cheer me on, yeah?'

Sohal watched her stride confidently towards the goalpost. He was amazed to see that Chip didn't object to Jaz joining in. He just nodded at her. *Maybe it's because Jaz stood up to him so bravely in PE*, Sohal thought. A pang of sadness filled his chest. He wished *he* was brave enough to join in the game.

Just as he was thinking this, he felt Ham Solo clamber on to his shoulder and tap his cheek. Ham was trying to show Sohal something.

'What is it, Ham?'

The hamster started frantically jumping up and down, pointing towards the football pitch.

Sohal groaned. 'Oh no, don't tell me *you* want to play too?'

Ham Solo was squealing and gesturing with both paws now. Sohal squinted towards where he was pointing, and then he saw it. At first he thought it was another football bouncing towards the pitch. Then he realized that the big dark blob was . . .

'ALONE!

NOOOOOOO!'

What was she doing? Sohal hurtled towards the football pitch with an incredibly excited Ham Solo scurrying behind him. Ham was hoping this was his chance to play in a real football game, like the ones he'd seen on TV. All those years of running in his hamster wheel were finally about to pay off!

Sohal went flying towards Alone and just before she could roll into the goal, landed on top of her with a mighty

thud.

Some of the other children began
cheering, but there was also a lot of booing.
When Sohal sat up and saw what he'd
landed on he realized why.

'OI, SHORTY!
Get yer mitts
OFF MY BALL!'

Chip Monk screamed across the pitch.

'That was MY GOAL
and YOU RUINED IT!'

Panic surged through Sohal's body.
If this was the football, then . . . where was
Alone? He scanned the pitch – and then

he saw her, now even bigger than before, bouncing excitedly towards some other children.

'Please play with me!' she squeaked. 'I love football!' But when the children saw her they screamed their heads off and ran for their lives.

'It's a GIANT RAT!'
'It's a TARANTULA!'
'It's a MONSTERRRRRRRR!'

Some children scrambled up a nearby tree. Others just ran away. Then some mean kids decided to bat Alone away with sticks, like a baseball. Sohal ran towards her with his arms out, desperately trying to catch her.

Then the worst possible thing happened. Alone landed on Chip Monk's head.

'AAAAAAAAAAAGH!'

Chip began whacking his head repeatedly and running around the pitch as if his bum was on fire. Everyone fell about laughing. No one had ever seen Chip Monk look so ridiculous.

After a few more head–whacks and hair-pulls, Chip finally managed to yank Alone off him. He hurled her across the playground, and Alone bounced and flipped along before rolling behind Sohal for refuge.

'OI, **CHUBBY CHOPS!**' Chip yelled, storming towards Sohal. 'That your pet?'

Sohal's throat tightened.

'**N-N-N-N-N-N-N-NO,**' he stuttered.

'First you mess up my goal, then you make me look like a complete and utter **IDIOT**! You're not gonna get away with this.'

Chip was standing very close to Sohal now. Suddenly he reached out, grabbed Sohal's cheeks, and started to pinch them.

Sohal winced. 'OW! Stop!'

A tear rolled down Sohal's cheek, but Chip didn't stop.

'Leave him! Stop it! Someone get a teacher!' Sohal could hear some kids shouting. But no one dared to pull Chip off him. Sohal could feel Alone pushing against his leg, whimpering behind him.

Just when Sohal thought he was really

going to cry, a small furry ball came whizzing out of nowhere and whacked Chip Monk right on the forehead.

'OWWWWWWW!'

Chip shrieked as he toppled backwards and on to the ground.

Sohal then realized what the small furry ball was. 'HAM SOLO!' he shouted.

His hamster was now standing triumphantly on Chip's chest, punching the air with his little fists.

Everyone in the playground cheered.

'You **hit** me, you little rat!' Chip snarled. He reached out with grubby, nail-bitten fingers and grabbed Ham Solo. The smell of Chip's filthy hand – a tangy mixture of bogies, wee and salt-and-vinegar crisps – was enough to make Ham Solo faint.

'Let him go!' Sohal shouted. 'You're squeezing him too hard!'

'Serves him right for nearly scratching my eyes out!' Chip shouted back. 'But fine. If you think I'm squeezing too hard . . .' He opened his fist and let Ham fall.

 Chapter

Just as Ham was about to land head first on the tarmac, another hand reached out and caught him. It was Jazmin's.

'Gotcha!' she yelled. 'You're OK now, lil dude.'

Jaz turned to Sohal, who looked like he was about to faint too, and carefully handed Ham back to him.

Sohal let out a giant sigh of relief, and felt Alone shrinking behind him.

'Thank you,' he said, still a bit breathless. 'Thank you, thank you, thank you!'

'And as for *you*,' Jaz said, looking at Chip. 'Leave my friend alone, Chip Monk.' Shaking her head, she added, 'You know, I can't believe your parents actually called you Chip Monk. CHIPMUNK! So what's the deal, you bully everyone else before they bully you? That's low, dude.'

For once Chip was silent. No one had EVER made Chip Monk silent before! Sohal felt a swell of pride. This VERY cool girl had just called him her *friend*!

'CHIP! MONK!' a voice boomed across the playground. It was Mrs Blunt, the headmistress, standing with her hands on her broad hips. 'COME TO MY OFFICE, NOW!'

Chip scampered towards her like a terrified, well, chipmunk. Sohal and his hamster watched wide-eyed, not quite believing what had just happened.

Then, as if she couldn't contain herself any longer, Alone stopped whimpering and popped up in front of Sohal.

'WHOA!'

Jaz yelped. 'What is THAT?'

Sohal gulped. He looked at Jazmin's big, kind eyes staring at Alone . . . and decided to trust her.

'Well, er . . . this is Alone. She's my . . . Worry.'

'OH! So that's the thing that was flying around the playground? I wondered why you were chasing it! Wow, dude, that's one **MASSIVE** Worry.'

Jaz took a step closer. She smiled at Alone, and Alone smiled back. Then, to Sohal's amazement, Jaz rummaged in her dress pocket . . . and pulled out a creature the size of a tennis ball. It had a purple Mohican and three big, blinking eyes.

'This is Loner,' she said. 'Sounds like he might be a cousin of yours, Alone. He can get pretty big too, sometimes. When I first started here he was the size of a donkey. I had to shove him in the stationery cupboard so no one would see him. But then I started making friends and little by little he shrank.'

'But how did you make friends?' Sohal said, amazed. 'I have no idea how to do it!'

Jaz laughed. 'You ARE doing it! You're talking to me, sharing your **ALIEN PET SHOP**™ cards, sharing your Worries . . . It's not always easy. People can be scary if you don't know them – but you're a brave dude, Sohal. And a funny one, too.'

Sohal hadn't meant to be funny. He wasn't sure he'd ever been funny in his entire life! But it felt nice to be laughing with Jaz.

For the rest of break time, Alone and Loner happily bounced around together. And for the rest of the day Sohal had a bright feeling inside him, knowing that Jaz

and her Worry were nearby.

By the end of the day Alone had shrunk
to an even smaller size than when she had
first appeared on Sohal's bed. She was so
small, in fact, that she snuck into his pencil
case, and fell fast asleep.

Later, when his mum and dad came to pick him up from school, Sohal had a big smile on his face for the first time in a long time. He told his mum and dad all about Jaz, but left out the bits about Chip, and Ham Solo and Alone. He didn't tell her about all his other Worries, either.

His mum grinned. 'That's great, darling! I'm so pleased you've made a friend.'

Sohal was pleased too, but as they walked home he started to remember Chip pinching his cheeks and nearly squeezing Ham Solo to death. Then he began to worry about going back to school tomorrow, and what might happen if Chip decided to get revenge on Sohal for getting him into trouble. And what would happen if Jaz decided she didn't want to be Sohal's friend after all? He'd have to go back to sitting on his own at break time, and his parents would be so disappointed.

Soon Sohal's worries were spinning around in his head again. By the time they had got home, he was so worried that he didn't even notice his rucksack beginning to strain at the zip . . . or the Worries tumbling out . . . or them scuttling up the stairs and charging into

HIS BEDROOM!

✿ chapter 12 ☆

'AAAAAAGH!'

Sohal yelled at the top of his voice.

His dad gasped. **'Oh blimey!'**
'Oh crikey!' Babs yelped.

His mum shrieked. 'What on EARTH?
What are *they*?'

'My Worries,' Sohal said, covering
his eyes.

Babs started flapping around, yanking the Worries off the bed. 'I'm awfully sorry about this!' she said in a fluster. 'Awfully sorry!'

'Hi!' Big waved, as he landed bottom first on the rug. 'Ooh, ouch!'

'Uh-oh, PARENTS!' Ang shouted from the lampshade she was currently swinging on. 'That usually means we're done for. **Kaput** . . . Are y'all gonna get mad and throw us outta the window?' she said anxiously.

'Cos I hear parents all the time telling their kids their Worries ain't real, that there's nothing to worry about, and blah-blah-blah. It's a load of baloney, though, cos we just end up coming back, even **bigger**!'

'Did someone say WINDOW?' Hurt shouted. 'I'm not going through any window! Not in *my* condition!'

'I'm not even sure I'd fit through that window,' said Alone.

'No, and I agree that's *not* the answer anyway,' said Sohal's dad. 'First I'm going to make us all sausages and mash, followed by my Super Ice-cream Sundae as a special treat.'

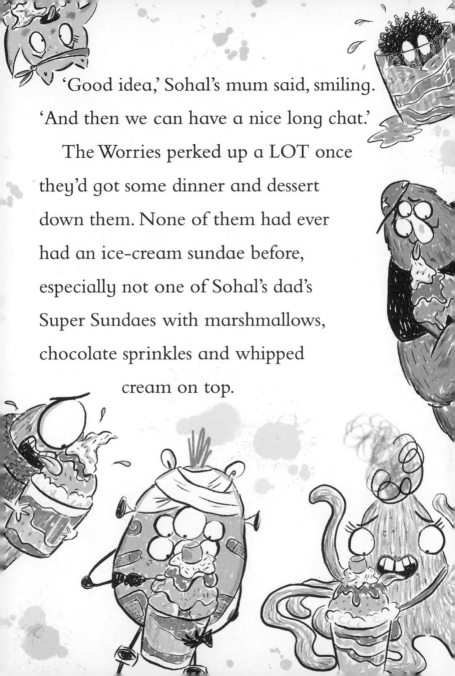

'Good idea,' Sohal's mum said, smiling. 'And then we can have a nice long chat.'

The Worries perked up a LOT once they'd got some dinner and dessert down them. None of them had ever had an ice-cream sundae before, especially not one of Sohal's dad's Super Sundaes with marshmallows, chocolate sprinkles and whipped cream on top.

Later, after a slightly chaotic but (in the end) relaxing bath time, everyone snuggled up on Sohal's bed – even Ham Solo. It was a bit of a squeeze. Mum and Dad asked Sohal and the Worries to tell them all about their day. Sohal's parents said that it was

important for Sohal to tell them about the difficult things that happened to him. That way, they could help him find a way to deal with the problems if they happened again. Talking about what happened would also make the memory of it less scary.

Sohal then told his parents about what had happened with Alone.

For the first time he felt able to say how his Worries had made him feel.

'I'm worried no one likes me,' he said. 'I feel . . . different to all the other kids at school.'

'We are **ALL** different, Sohal,' Mum said. 'And that's what makes us brilliant. No two people are ever the same!'

'Exactly!' Dad said. 'And that's why sometimes it can be tricky making friends. But you did such a big brave thing today, Sohal. Even with all your Worries running around, you managed to talk to Jaz and make a new friend!'

'Yes, and I bet there are lots more people who would like to be your friend once they got to know you,' Mum added.

'But why do they never talk to me then?' Sohal said sadly.

'Well, maybe they tried and you were

too shy to notice,' Mum said thoughtfully. 'Or maybe they haven't yet because they're scared, like you.'

'Yes – sometimes it's really hard to tell what people are actually thinking or feeling,' Dad said. 'You can't always rely on how they look, or how they act.'

'Ugh, I KNOW,' said Sohal. 'It's **SO confusing**!'

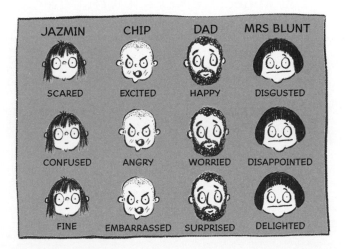

Mum laughed. 'It is! That's why it's great you're being so honest with us about your feelings now, Sohal. We mustn't hide our worries away or try to deal with them on our own. So, next time your Worries appear, you bring them to us and we'll help you keep them as small and as well behaved as possible. Agreed?'

Sohal smiled, feeling so much better. 'Agreed.'

'Good. Right, then!' said Dad. 'I think it's time for a nice bedtime story, followed by a good night's sleep.'

The Worries then snuggled under the quilt

with Sohal and listened to his dad read to them. Sohal felt safe and comforted, and he was so glad he'd spoken to his parents.

Finally, with only one night light on, he and the Worries sank into a deep and lovely sleep.

Chapter 13

The next morning, Sohal's mum woke him up early.

'Agh, what's happening?' grumbled Big, pulling the quilt over his head. 'I was **SLEEPING**!'

'Time for schoooool!' Mum sang.

'Not SCHOOL!' Hurt whinged. 'It's far too dangerous!'

Babs sprang awake and began whipping all the Worries out of bed with her tentacles.

'Come on!
Chop-chop!'

She yanked back the bedcovers. 'Ya heard
what she said. School! We can't be late. Ya
know how all of ya HATE being late.'
'OOOOOOH, everyone staring at me!'
Alone moaned. 'No
thank you!'

AAAGH!

'And that frowning boss lady Blunt, who looks like she's gonna explode any minute? Uh-uh!' Ang said, folding her arms defiantly. 'I do NOT wanna be there when *that* bomb goes off. No way!

'And your name going in the LATE REGISTER!' squeaked Fail.

'For EVERRRRR!'

Sohal sat up in bed and watched them all, flapping and huffing and talking over one other. He put his hands over his ears and shouted:

'STOP!

**I DON'T WANT ANY OF YOU TO
COME TO SCHOOL!'**

The Worries fell silent.

Sohal went on. 'I've had enough. I just want you to

GO AWAY!'

Now the Worries looked hurt.

'Sohal,' said Mum, 'I thought we talked about this last night. You can't run away from your Worries. Hiding from them won't make them go away.'

'But what about Chip and his gang?' Sohal asked. 'What if they pick on me and the Worries?'

'I think you'll find everyone has Worries, sweetie,' his mum said, stroking his hair. 'You might be surprised to see what happens if you *don't* hide yours.'

Sohal slowly nodded, and the Worries looked relieved. In fact, by the time they'd eaten breakfast, Sohal's Worries were so relaxed they were small enough to pack into his rucksack.

On the way to school Sohal thought hard about what his mum had said. When he got to the school gates, he made a decision. Sohal crouched down and unzipped his rucksack. His furry Worries stared back at him with their big, funny eyes.

'Right, you lot, we're going to do this one step at a time,' he said, reaching his hand in and pulling out Alone. 'Come on, you. No more hiding. Mum's right.'

Alone wriggled out of Sohal's hand and bounced excitedly on to his head.

'Hi!' came a friendly voice from behind him.

Sohal turned and was pleased to see it was Jaz.

He blushed. 'Oh, hi!'

'I see you've got a cool new hat,' Jaz said, laughing and pointing at Alone.

'Ha, yeah. I'm trying not to hide her any more.'

'That's brave, dude. Nice one,' Jaz said, thumping him on the arm.

Sohal knew Jaz meant it in a friendly way, but it was confusing! It was a good example of what his dad had said – that people's behaviour didn't always match their real feelings.

'Ha ha. So, er . . . where's Loner then?' Sohal asked as he and Jaz walked down the corridor.

'Didn't want to come to school today.'
She shrugged. 'Maybe it's cos I've got a new friend,' she said, smiling at Sohal.

Sohal smiled back – then suddenly

stopped

dead

still.

Chip Monk was coming down the corridor towards them!

Sohal really wanted to take Alone off his head and shove her back into his rucksack, but he resisted with all his might. He thought again about what his mum had said, and now he had Jaz's words in his head too. *That's brave, dude. Nice one.* That made him feel even braver.

Chip marched up and stood right in front of Sohal. He stared at Alone, who stared blankly back at him.

Jaz quickly stepped in between them. 'What do you want now, Chip?' she said, attempting her meanest face (which actually wasn't mean at all).

Sohal realized Chip looked sheepish. In fact, he almost looked . . . *scared*.

Then Chip lifted up his jumper to reveal three little creatures clinging to his vest. They looked a lot like Sohal's Worries, only not as furry or colourful.

'Uh, these are my Worries. This is Tough Guy, Stupid and, um . . . Sad.' He put them down on the floor carefully. 'Mrs Blunt told me I have to apologize to you. So, er, I got 'em to do a rap. OK, you guys, hit it.

One, two, three, four . . .'

I'm **TOUGH GUY**, *worried about being* **weak**.
My **FISTS** *do the talkin' cos I don't like to speak.*
I get into fights nearly every day,
But I promised Mrs Blunt that I'm gonna **change my ways**.

Yo, I'm **STUPID**, *the biggest* **class clown** *in town.*
So no one sees my mistakes **I fool around**.

124

I'd like to be clever but
I'm **SCARED** of numbers.
Letters and words make me feel
even dumber.

My name's **SAD**, and I'm no good at **rappin'**.
I'd just like to say I'm sorry for **scrappin'**,
Especially to Sohal and his hamster too,
And everyone we've **bullied** in Year Two.

'Oh, wow,' Jaz said when Chip's Worries had finished. 'I had no idea you were worried about being weak or stupid or sad. To be honest, I thought you were just mean, dude. But that was . . . pretty cool.'

Alone bounced down from Sohal's shoulder, even smaller now. She inspected Chip's Worries like a dog sniffing bums.

'Yeah, that was pretty cool,' Sohal muttered, staring at the creatures.

'Thanks,' Chip said awkwardly. 'And sorry again, Sohal. I'd better get goin'. We've got a lot of other kids to apologize to.'

'Thanks, Chip. Bye!' Jaz said, raising one hand.

They watched Chip lumber off down

the corridor, his Worries scampering ahead of him. 'Wow, that was . . . unexpected,' said Jaz.

'Yeah,' Sohal said. 'Very! I mean, I had no idea Chip Monk actually *had* Worries.'

'Or that he'd ever say **SORRY**!' Jaz laughed. 'It must be the first time in his **entire LIFE**!'

'I guess my mum was right,' Sohal said. 'Everyone *does* have Worries. I'm more normal than I thought.'

'Well, my mum loves saying things like, "There's no such thing as normal."' Jaz grinned, looking down at their Worries. 'I guess we're all a bit strange really!'

Chapter 14

Sohal's Worries stayed in his rucksack for most of the day. Sometimes one or two would pop up their little heads, but the rest

of the time they
just snoozed.
Sohal was
able to concentrate on
what he was doing, and sometimes he even
completely forgot about his Worries.

At break time, the Scaredy Cats made a comeback on the football pitch. Even Chip agreed to join them. It turned out he and Sohal made a pretty good team, with Sohal scoring his first-ever goal! It was his proudest moment at school.

That afternoon, when his dad came to pick him up, Sohal told him all about his day. When Dad said he could invite Jaz round for tea, Sohal thought he might actually **BURST** with happiness.

While Sohal and Jaz played together, so did their Worries. They were both having such a nice time that, at first, they didn't notice their Worries sneak off. Then Sohal realized how much *calmer* he felt. His thoughts weren't racing, his body felt lighter, and he didn't have a sick feeling in his stomach.

'Hang on,' said Sohal. 'Where *are* the Worries?'

Jaz looked up from their **ALIEN PET SHOP**™ cards, frowned and looked around. 'I'm not sure. Wait, do you hear that?'

Sohal held his breath and listened. He thought he heard some scratching and scuffling noises coming from inside his toy cupboard.

He and Jazmin crept closer and . . .

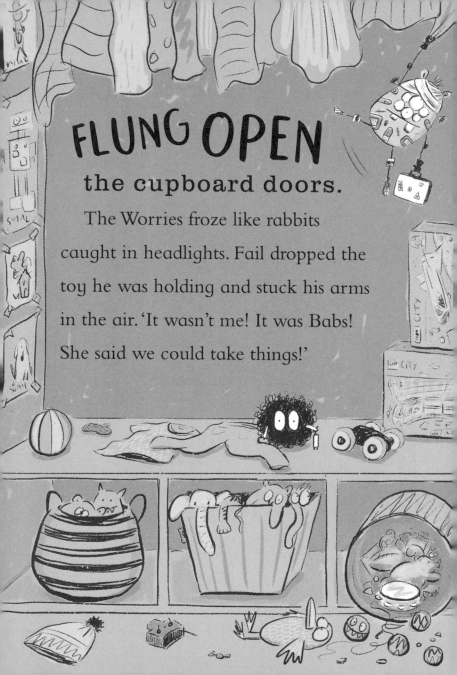

FLUNG OPEN
the cupboard doors.

The Worries froze like rabbits caught in headlights. Fail dropped the toy he was holding and stuck his arms in the air. 'It wasn't me! It was Babs! She said we could take things!'

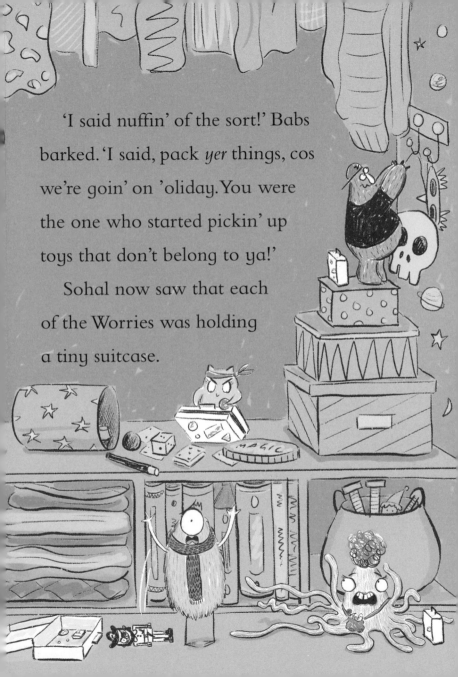

'I said nuffin' of the sort!' Babs
barked. 'I said, pack *yer* things, cos
we're goin' on 'oliday. You were
the one who started pickin' up
toys that don't belong to ya!'

Sohal now saw that each
of the Worries was holding
a tiny suitcase.

'You're going on *holiday*?' Sohal asked, confused.

'I'm sorryyyyy!' squeaked Alone, who was incredibly small now. 'I'm really gonna miss you, but you don't need me at the moment.'

Sohal looked at Alone's big eyes and realized she was right. *Maybe a holiday would do the Worries good*, he thought. *And maybe it will do ME good too!*

'Come on then,
     ya little MONSTERS,'

Babs shouted. 'Let's get a move on. Say goodbye to Sohal. He's doin' just fine.'

'Can I just *borrow* this lil fella?' Big said,

picking up a teddy bear that was almost the same size as him.

Sohal laughed. 'OK, sure.'

It was the special teddy that usually helped Sohal fall asleep, but he realized he hadn't needed it the last few nights.

The other Worries started waving toys in Sohal's face.

'Oh, oh, can I borrow this?'

'And this?'

'**PLEASE** let me take this!'

'You can take whatever you like,' Sohal said kindly.

'But NOT our **ALIEN PET SHOP**™ cards,' Jaz said firmly, stopping a very guilty-looking Loner and making him empty his suitcase.

'OK, man, you got me. Doh.'

Once the Worries had squeezed all they could into their suitcases, Babs marched them out of Sohal's bedroom and down the stairs. Sohal's mum and dad stuck their heads out of the living room to see what all the noise was.

'The Worries are going on holiday!' Sohal explained.

'Oh, right! How lovely!' Mum said.

'Anywhere nice?' Dad asked.

'*Everywhere* nice!' Babs replied. 'We might do a world tour, dependin' on how things go.

I'm sure we'll be back soon, though.'

'Well, hopefully not *too* soon!' Dad said, laughing.

'Yes, you lot just . . . take your time!' Mum said. 'I've heard New Zealand is lovely.'

Then the Worries gathered round and gave Sohal a big hug.

'Bye,' Sohal said, squeezing them tight. 'It was . . . weird getting to know you. But I'm glad I did. I'm gonna . . . miss you, I guess?'

The Worries clung on to Sohal even tighter and cooed:

'AAAAAAW, SOHAL!'

Jaz high-fived Loner. 'Well, see ya, dude. Good to see you've got some friends now.'

'Yeah, you too, dude!' He grinned. 'Remember, keep jammin'!'

Jaz, Sohal, and his mum and dad waved the Worries off as they toddled down the road.

'Hang on a minute,' Sohal said, frowning. 'Where's Ang?'

Just as he said it, they heard a shriek and the rumbling of wheels behind them. They turned to see Ang whizzing down the path on a skateboard, swiftly pursued by the cat.

'ALL ABOARD!!'

Ang yelled. Just in the nick of time the Worries leaped on to the passing skateboard and went flying off down the road, waving their furry arms in the air.

'SEND US A POSTCARD!' Sohal shouted.

And they did.